UP AND DOWN THE MOUNTAIN

Helping Children Cope with Parental Alcoholism

story by Pamela Leib Higgins
illustrated by Gail Zawacki

New Horizon Press
Far Hills, New Jersey

New Horizon Press
P.O. Box 669
Far Hills, NJ 07931

Higgins, Pamela Lieb
    Up and Down the Mountain: Helping Children Cope with Parental Alcoholism

    Illustrated by Gail Zawacki

Library of Congress Catalog Card Number: 94-66763
ISBN-13: 978-0-88282-133-7

SMALL HORIZONS
A Division of New Horizon Press

2017 2016 2015 2014 2013   2 3 4 5 6

Printed in the U.S.A.

I sit quietly at the breakfast table. Today I will be graduating from the sixth grade. I will put on the new pink-flowered dress which is hanging in my closet. The dress has a bow on the back and big, puffy sleeves.

I will walk across the assembly room at our school and proudly shake hands with Mr. Healey, our principal.

Yesterday, our class had a rehearsal to make sure that everyone knew what to do. Mr. Healey kept reminding us to smile. He said that graduating from the sixth grade should be a happy day. The people in the· audience will want to see us smiling.

I know what I will be doing. I will be looking for Daddy.

So many times before, when something important was happening at my school, Mom would be there. Jake, my little brother, would sit beside her.

On the other side of Mom, though, would be an empty chair. She would put coats on it to make it look less empty, but it was still empty. It was the chair being saved for Daddy, just in case he came.

    All the time I've been in elementary school, Daddy has only shown up twice. One time he fell down, and some people had to help him up. The other time he went to sleep. He started snoring so loudly that people turned around to stare at him. My face turned red. I remember wishing he had stayed home.

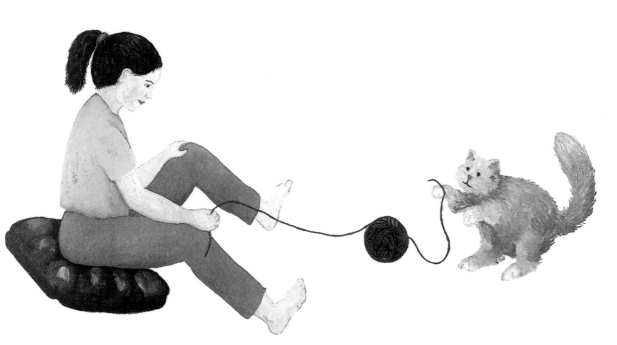

Now I am eleven years old, and I understand that Daddy is an alcoholic. That means that he drinks too much liquor and does not always act the way other fathers do. I wish that someone had explained these things to me when I was little. So many times I felt sad growing up. I wanted to make everything better, but I never could.

My kitten was my best friend. His name was Cooper, and I played with him a lot. He understood how I felt.

I remember a birthday party. I was probably turning four or five. Mom had put up lots of big balloons to decorate the house. She dressed me in a blue party dress with white, shiny clouds on it.

Daddy looked happy. He was holding me on his lap, and we were laughing about something. I felt safe. I felt like the luckiest child in the world to have such a wonderful father.

Then my brother started fussing. He was in his baby rocker. He cried harder and harder. Mom came in from the kitchen, holding a dinner plate in one hand. She said something which made Daddy angry. Suddenly, he sat me on the floor. He stood up and walked toward the door, knocking the dinner plate down as he passed my mother.

Kernels of corn flew in all directions. Yellow spots were on the walls and on the ceiling. My Mom and my brother Jake were crying. I thought I had done something wrong, even though Mom told me I hadn't.

When I was about six, I decided that Daddy was like a roller-coaster on a mountain. His mood would go up, up and up for a while. He'd be full of energy, hugging Mom and playing with Jake and me.

During these times, he would take the family to wonderful places. The four of us would go to the movies or to carnivals.

Sometimes we would drive to the stadium to watch Daddy's favorite football team. I tried to learn a lot about football. I wanted Daddy to be proud of me, but I don't know if he was.

There are rose bushes in front of our house. Taking care of the roses was something special I did alone with Daddy. When I was younger, he used to let me hold the big garden scissors. Then he would put his rough hands over mine. Together, we would cut and cut until all the long branches were short again.

Mom would wave at us from the house. I loved working in the roses with my father. We were happy.

But our family was never happy for long. I always knew when the bad times were coming. If Daddy drank for a long time, he would finally go over the top of his invisible mountain—just like a roller-coaster—and then race down the other side. It was scary whenever that happened.

All I had to do was look at Daddy's face, and I knew that we were sliding down with him. That's when things seemed crazy and out of control.

When those bad times came, we would still go places.
They weren't fun anymore, though.

One night I sat next to Daddy in a restaurant. He was
talking loudly. He told Jake to run to the other side of the
crowded room. Then he grabbed a dinner roll out of the bread
basket. Daddy called to Jake that a football was coming into
the end-zone, and then he threw the roll across the restaurant.
The other people watched the roll sail over their heads.

No matter what, our family always protected Daddy. We would apologize for him and help him into the back seat of the car.

At home, we would put him on the couch. I'd take off his shoes, then go upstairs to get his old football blanket.

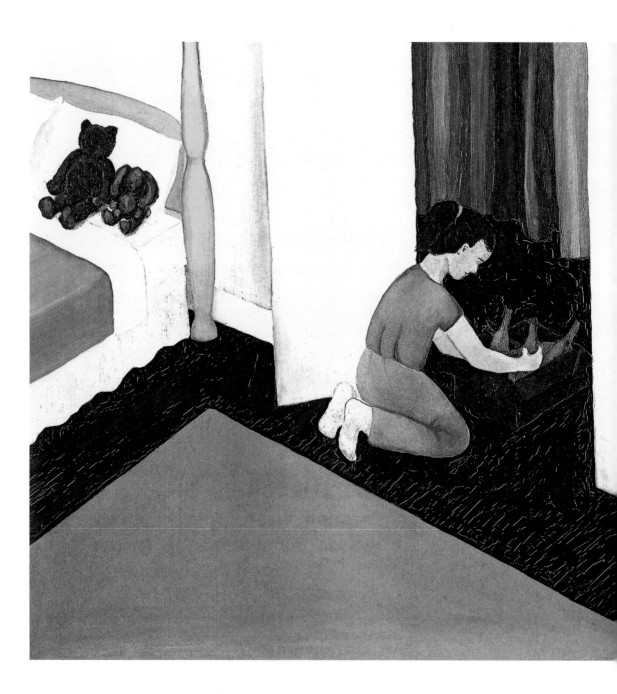

I felt so helpless and alone. Mom didn't like talking about what was wrong with Daddy. I don't think she knew what to do. I thought that if I was good enough—if I tried hard enough—Daddy would be happy all the time and not need to drink.

I begged him to stop. I even tried to hide his bottles in my closet. But he would just buy more.

No matter how hard I tried, he still drank.

I became afraid to invite friends over to my house because I never knew how Daddy would behave.

I used to sit by the window with Cooper and watch the other children play outside. Mom tried to get me to play with them, but I wouldn't. What if the children wanted to come inside my house? Then they might see Daddy drinking too much.

I just watched them play from my window.

At last, this year, things began to change for me. My principal, Mr. Healey, stopped me in the hall at school. He asked if I would talk to someone about the problems in my family. At first, I didn't want to. How could a stranger possibly offer me any help?

Mr. Healey thought that I should give his friend a chance. He said that her name was Cathy, she was a counselor and that she knew a lot about alcoholism—the disease my Daddy has.

The first day I went to see Cathy, my stomach felt awful. I couldn't stop biting my nails. I didn't know what to say. I didn't know where to begin.

We talked a little about school and other things. Before I realized it, though, I was telling her everything. She understood what I was saying and how I felt. It was nice to speak with her.

I have learned so much in the last year. I have learned that alcoholism is a disease, and that Daddy doesn't know how to stop drinking. It would be very hard for him to do without lots and lots of help.

I have also found out that there are many other families with the same problem. I don't feel that I need to hide it or be ashamed anymore. I've even started to make some new friends.

Cathy says there is help for Daddy, but that he has to decide if he wants it. Daddy is the only one with the power to change himself. I'm beginning to understand that when he drinks, it's not my fault. I shouldn't blame myself.

Now I am able to think more about my homework. My teacher told Mom that I'm doing better in school.

Mom and my brother Jake have also spoken to Cathy. We've learned that when Daddy goes down the dark side of the mountain, he probably doesn't want to be there. He doesn't mean to hurt us, either. The alcohol is doing that, and Daddy has no control over alcohol.

We want him to realize how much he needs help. Maybe someday he will get better. I really hope so.

For now, I have found things that I like to do. Ice skating is my favorite! I can almost do a full spin.

For my birthday, I told my father that I wished he would talk to Cathy, just once. I couldn't believe it, but he did. I came in at the end of their talk, and Cathy asked me to tell Daddy my feelings. I cried. I told him how much I loved him and that I wanted him to stop drinking.

We went to the park for ice cream afterwards.

For the first time, I thought that Daddy was really listening to me.

Now it's graduation day. I run upstairs, put on my dress, and brush my hair.

Lying on my dresser is a beautiful pink rose. It matches my dress. It must be from Daddy!

I put my hair in a ponytail, then carefully slip the pretty rose inside the rubber band.

Mom is waiting in the den with Jake. My brother is dressed up in his dark green jacket and tie.

I ask for Daddy, but I see that his car is gone. I begin to feel nervous. I am so afraid that he has left to go drinking.

My hands are shaking. I can hardly buckle my white shoes. Mom leans over to help me.

She says, as always, that we will save a seat for Daddy.

We are at school now. My friends and I are walking down the aisle of our school's assembly room.

Music is playing. Sunlight floods through the big windows.

I look out across the audience and I smile. I really smile. Daddy is there, sitting tall and straight and proud in the chair next to Mom and Jake. I reach back to touch the rose in my hair. I keep walking and nobody has to remind me to smile today.

— THE END —

TIPS FOR CHILDREN

1. If your parent drinks too much, remember it is not your fault. Alcoholism is an illness. Don't blame yourself.

2. Your parent's alcoholism doesn't mean he or she doesn't love you. Sometimes when people drink, they are unable to show that they care because of their illness.

3. Think about ways you can show your parents that you care.

4. Do not be afraid to let your parents know if they have hurt your feelings.

5. Share your hurt feelings with a grown-up you trust. Talk to a teacher or school counselor to help you feel better and learn more about your parent's illness.

6. Do not be ashamed. Your parent is not the only one suffering from alcoholism. Lots of kids are going through the same problems.

7. Take care of yourself. Know that you are a good person and you deserve to be treated kindly. If your alcoholic parent acts like a bully, tell someone you trust that you need help.

8. Trust your feelings. When your parent drinks too much, he or she can act just like a stranger. If you don't feel safe near a person who has had too much to drink, stay out of his or her way or call a grown-up who can help.

TIPS FOR PARENTS AND TEACHERS OF KIDS WITH ALCOHOLIC PARENTS

1. It is important for children to know that there are adults around with whom they can talk about their parent's alcoholism.

2. Be supportive and listen closely to what the child says about how his or her parent's alcoholism makes him or her feel.

3. Educate children about alcoholism. Tell them that it is an illness and that the alcoholic parent is sick.

4. Talk to your children about alcoholism and let them know the illness is not their fault and it doesn't mean the alcoholic parent does not love them. Rather, alcoholic parents are sometimes unable to show their love because of their illness.

5. Encourage children to focus on schoolwork and not on worrying about their parent's alcoholism.

6. If the children of an alcoholic parent have to assume adult responsibilities because of their parent's drinking, create opportunities for them to be children.

7. Seek professional counseling to help a child deal with the embarrassment, depression or anxiety that can stem from having an alcoholic parent.

8. Have a plan for if the alcoholic parent creates serious problems or becomes violent; let children know where to go and what to do.

9. Be a good example.